Dedications

This story is dedicated to Maile, the personification of Aloha.
She inspires with her kindness and boundless heart.
Always, always helping everyone around her, she is selfless in her
service. We love you Mai. You are a blessing in all our lives.
–Dani Hickman

I'm dedicating this to the endangered sea creatures.
–Sudipta Dasgupta

ISLAND HERITAGE™
PUBLISHING
A DIVISION OF THE MADDEN CORPORATION

94-411 Kō'aki Street
Waipahu, Hawai'i 96797-2806
Orders: (800) 468-2800
Information: (808) 564-8800
Fax: (808) 564-8877
welcometotheislands.com

ISBN: 1-61710-399-3
First Edition, Second Printing-2019
COP 191601

TAKO
Lends a Helping Hand

Written By Jenna and Dani Hickman
Illustrated by Sudipta Dasgupta

ISLAND HERITAGE™
PUBLISHING

Tako and her Mama lived deep in the ocean near the big pink coral reef. One day after breakfast, Mama asked, "Tako, will you help me get some *limu* for lunch today?"

"Yes, Mama. I will help you," said Tako. She started toward the edge of the reef where the *limu* grew, humming to herself. *I know, I know, I know I can take time to lend a helping hand.*

3

On the way, Tako met Crab.
"Oh good," said Crab. "I'm glad I found you! Remember you said you would help me find shells so that I can make a necklace for Seal's birthday."

"Of course, Crab! I will help you," said Tako.
I know, I know, I know I can
Take time to lend a helping hand.

5

Tako began looking for shells and forgot about getting *limu* for Mama.

Soon Crab and Tako came upon Whale, who was very upset. "What's wrong, Whale?" asked Tako.

7

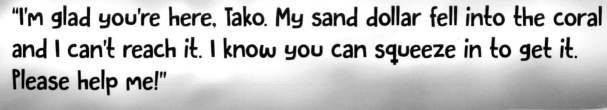

"I'm glad you're here, Tako. My sand dollar fell into the coral and I can't reach it. I know you can squeeze in to get it. Please help me!"

8

"Of course, Whale. I will help you," said Tako.
I know, I know, I know I can
Take time to lend a helping hand.

9

When Whale and Tako
got near the coral, Eel
popped his head out.

"Tako, Tako, I need your help! My favorite
sea sponge got caught on a buoy above
the water. Can you reach up and grab it
for me?" asked Eel.

"Of course, Eel. I will help you," said Tako.
I know, I know, I know I can
Take time to lend a helping hand.

Tako followed Eel to the surface.
As Eel and Tako swam along, Honu rushed up.
"There you are Tako. I've been looking everywhere for you.
Dolphin is tangled in a net! I need your help!"

"Of course I'll help you," said Tako.
*I know, I know, I know I can
Take time to lend a helping hand.*

But before Tako could swim off, Eel said "I thought you were helping *me*, Tako." Whale swam up and said, "Tako why did you swim away? I thought you were helping *me*."

Crab finally caught up, all out of breath. "Tako, *(wheeze)* you swim too fast. *(wheeze)* I thought you were helping *me*."

14

Then Tako saw the *limu* patch and remembered she was also supposed to help Mama. "Oh no," thought Tako. "How can I help everyone?"

15

Mama asked for *limu*, Crab needs help finding shells,
Whale can't reach into the coral for her sand dollar,
Eel can't get his sea sponge, and Dolphin is trapped in the net.

"I could do things in order and start with Mama's *limu*. But Dolphin is in serious trouble! Maybe there's another way...." Tako frowned and scratched her head.

"I know!" she said, "Here's what we can do: "Crab, would you please gather *limu* for Mama? Eel, would you squeeze into the coral and help Whale get her sand dollar? Whale, will you bump the buoy and knock Eel's sea sponge back into the water?

I'm going to go with Honu and help Dolphin."

"When we're done, we'll all meet here and help Crab look for shells. How does that sound?"
"YES!" They all cheered.

We know, we know, we know we can
Take time to lend a helping hand.
Tako, Crab, Whale, and Eel rushed off to help.

When they were finished, they hunted shells with Crab and found so many that Crab had enough to make a necklace for each of them.

Tako went home and enjoyed a delicious *limu* salad while she told Mama about all the ways her friends had helped.

23

The End